THIS BOOK BELONGS TO

D1195893

PELLEGRINIS BAR

HILL OF CONTENT

For Maureen and Robert

Found in Melbourne

a counting adventure

Melbourne

Joanne O'Callaghan

illustrated by Kori Song

ALLEN&UNWIN

SYDNEY•MELBOURNE•AUCKLAND•LONDON

1

One giant mouth, that's the way inside.
Look, it's Luna Park and the roller-coaster ride.

2

Two people sing and dance in the show,
To beautiful music from the orchestra below.

3

Three trams moving along in a line
On Princes Bridge, and down past the Shrine.

4

Four bicycles on the path by the bay.
A ship to Tasmania sailing away.

5

Five hands touch the huge Waterwall.
Let's wander the galleries and the Great Hall.

6

Six koalas hug a gum tree
On the Great Ocean Road, down by the sea.

7

Seven carriages on the railway track,
Puffing through the forest and all the way back.

QUEEN VICTORIA MARKET

NEW
Honey & walnut
Ice-Cream
NOW
Available!

8

Eight kinds of ice cream, how will we pick?
Chocolate or mango? Let's take a lick!

9

Nine magpies follow their favourite team,
A Grand Final win is a very big dream.

10

Ten clocks at the station where we meet for the train.
Bring an umbrella, it could start to rain!

11

Eleven fairy penguins, all black and white,
Parading every sunset, what a happy sight.

12

Twelve fancy cakes all ready for High Tea.
Come in and share some pavlova with me.

100

One hundred butterflies flutter at the zoo,
It's home to a few hungry caterpillars too.

1000

One thousand triangles in Federation Square,
And a Chinese lion is dancing there.

1,000,000

One million stories, ready to share,
In the grand reading room, just up the stairs.

There's so much to see and new friends to meet,
In the park, on the tram, or out in the street.
Melbourne is where I want to be.
Marvellous Melbourne is a place for me!

Melbourne Sights Found in this Book

Luna Park
This historic amusement park is located in St Kilda and was opened in 1912. The most famous of Luna Park's attractions is the Great Scenic Railway, an iconic sight and the oldest continually operating wooden roller-coaster in the world.

The Shrine of Remembrance
The Shrine of Remembrance was unveiled in 1934 and is a site of annual Anzac Day (25 April) and Remembrance Day (11 November) Services. The Shrine honours those who have served with and alongside Australia in armed conflicts and peacekeeping operations.

Princess Theatre
Located on Spring Street in Melbourne's East End Theatre District, the Princess Theatre is one of several grand theatres in the heart of Melbourne. The Princess Theatre hosts performances from around the world.

Princes Bridge
Princes Bridge was opened in 1888. It crosses the Yarra River near Flinders Street Station, and remains one of the city's best known landmarks.

Port Phillip and Port Melbourne
Port Phillip is home to beaches, coastal parks, yacht clubs, piers, and many playgrounds. An extensive bicycle path follows the coastline of Port Phillip. Ships depart daily from Port Melbourne for Tasmania.

The National Gallery of Victoria
The National Gallery of Victoria, popularly known as the NGV, was founded in 1861. It is Australia's oldest and most visited art museum. The St Kilda Road building, designed by Sir Roy Grounds, opened in 1968 and features the much-loved Waterwall entrance.

Great Ocean Road
The Great Ocean Road follows one of the world's most scenic coastlines. The road is 243 kilometres long and features forests that are home to koalas and many other Australian animals.

Puffing Billy Railway
Puffing Billy is an historic steam train, which takes you through the magnificent forest landscape of the Dandenong Ranges. Since 1900, the efforts of volunteers have kept Puffing Billy puffing for all to enjoy.

Queen Victoria Market
Queen Victoria Market is a vibrant and bustling inner-city market, where you can shop for fruit and vegetables, local and imported gourmet foods – and ice cream!

Melbourne Cricket Ground
The Melbourne Cricket Ground, popularly known as the MCG, is Australia's largest sports stadium, and one of the world's greatest sporting venues. It is home to the Melbourne Cricket Club and regularly hosts cricket matches and Australian Rules football games.

Flinders Street Station
Flinders Street Station is a cultural icon of Melbourne on the corner of Flinders and Swanston Streets. It serves the metropolitan rail network and was completed in 1910. The historic station was repainted in 2018 to restore its original colours.

Phillip Island
At dusk every evening, a parade of little penguins can be seen waddling along a Phillip Island beach to their burrows in the sand dunes.

Hopetoun Tea Rooms
The Block Arcade in Collins Street has been home to the Hopetoun Tea Rooms for more than a century. The mouth-watering window display of beautiful cakes is hard to walk past.

Federation Square
Opened in 2002, Federation Square is a major public square opposite Flinders Street Station. It hosts major cultural attractions, events, tourism experiences, restaurants, and specialty stores. Triangular shapes are a key architectural feature of this public square.

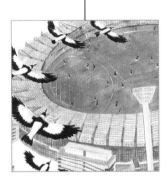

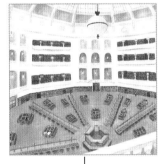

Melbourne Zoo
The Royal Melbourne Zoological Gardens, commonly known as Melbourne Zoo, opened in 1862. It is Australia's oldest zoo and home to more than 320 animal species. The Butterfly House is an enchanting tropical glasshouse, full of hundreds of spectacular native Australian butterflies.

State Library of Victoria
The State Library of Victoria is Australia's oldest public library and was one of the first free public libraries in the world. The La Trobe Reading Room is a magnificent domed reading room in the heart of the library. The impressive octagonal space was designed to hold more than a million books.

The Royal Exhibition Building and Carlton Gardens
The Royal Exhibition Building was built for the Melbourne International Exhibition in 1880–81. In 1901, it hosted the opening of the first Parliament of Australia. It is still in use as an exhibition venue, and sits in the picturesque Carlton Gardens.

Joanne O'Callaghan

Joanne made a buoyant debut as a children's author with her bestseller *My Hong Kong*, illustrated by woodblock print artist Ralph Kiggell. Her other books include *The Swimmers* and *Found in Hong Kong*, both beautifully and delicately illustrated by Kori Song, an award-winning Chinese artist.

Following 12 years in Hong Kong, Joanne and her family moved to Melbourne. *Found in Melbourne* celebrates her new home as well as Chinese-Australian friendships and connections.

www.joanneocallaghan.com

Kori Song

Kori's beautifully composed and observant illustrations reflect her interest in the relationship between cities and those who live in them. Kori's first book, *Cicada*, was a Winner in the Sun Hung Kai Properties Young Writers' Debut Competition in 2013. Kori graduated from Sichuan Fine Arts Institute, in Chongqing, China.

Kori loves Melbourne's trams, trees, and the variety of birds that can be found in the city. She lives in Hong Kong with her husband Bong and a cat named Go-Go.

www.korisong.com

CITY OF MELBOURNE

Supported by the City of Melbourne Arts Grants Program

First published by Allen & Unwin in 2018

Allen & Unwin
83 Alexander Street
Crows Nest NSW 2065
Australia
Phone: (61 2) 8425 0100
Email: info@allenandunwin.com
Web: www.allenandunwin.com

A catalogue record for this
book is available from the
National Library of Australia

ISBN 978 1 76052 341 1 (English)
ISBN 978 1 76063 296 0 (Simplified Chinese)

For teaching resources, explore www.allenandunwin.com/resources/for-teachers

Cover design by Sandra Nobes
Cover illustrations by Kori Song
Text design and typesetting by Sandra Nobes
This book was printed in May 2018 by C&C Offset Printing Co. Ltd, China

3 5 7 9 10 8 6 4 2